Miriam's MAGICAL CREATURE FILES
The Discovery of Dragons

 **Follow Miriam on all of her adventures!**

CASE #1 The Truth About the Tooth Fairy

CASE #2 The Discovery of Dragons

CASE #3 The Mystery of the Mermaid

Miriam's MAGICAL CREATURE FILES
The Discovery of Dragons

by Leah Cypess ♥ illustrated by Sarah Lynne Reul

Amulet Books ♥ New York

PUBLISHER'S NOTE: This is a work of fiction. Names, characters, places, and incidents are either the product of the author's imagination or used fictitiously, and any resemblance to actual persons, living or dead, business establishments, events, or locales is entirely coincidental.

Cataloging-in-Publication Data has been applied for and may be obtained from the Library of Congress.

Hardcover ISBN 978-1-4197-7242-9
Paperback ISBN 978-1-4197-7243-6
eISBN 979-8-88707-229-6

Text © 2025 Leah Cypess
Illustrations © 2025 Sarah Lynne Reul
Book design by Charice Silverman

Published in 2025 by Amulet Books, an imprint of ABRAMS. All rights reserved. No portion of this book may be reproduced, stored in a retrieval system, or transmitted in any form or by any means, mechanical, electronic, photocopying, recording, or otherwise, without written permission from the publisher.

Printed and bound in the United States
10 9 8 7 6 5 4 3 2 1

ABRAMS is represented in the UK and Europe by Abrams & Chronicle Books, 1 West Smithfield, London EC1A 9JU and Média-Participations, 57 rue Gaston Tessier, 75166 Paris, France. abramsandchronicle.co.uk and media-participations.com
info@abramsandchronicle.co.uk

Amulet Books® is a registered trademark of Harry N. Abrams, Inc.

Images courtesy of shutterstock.com: *washi tape*, Kbiscuit; *notes and clips*, Your Local Llamacorn.

ABRAMS The Art of Books
195 Broadway, New York, NY 10007
abramsbooks.com

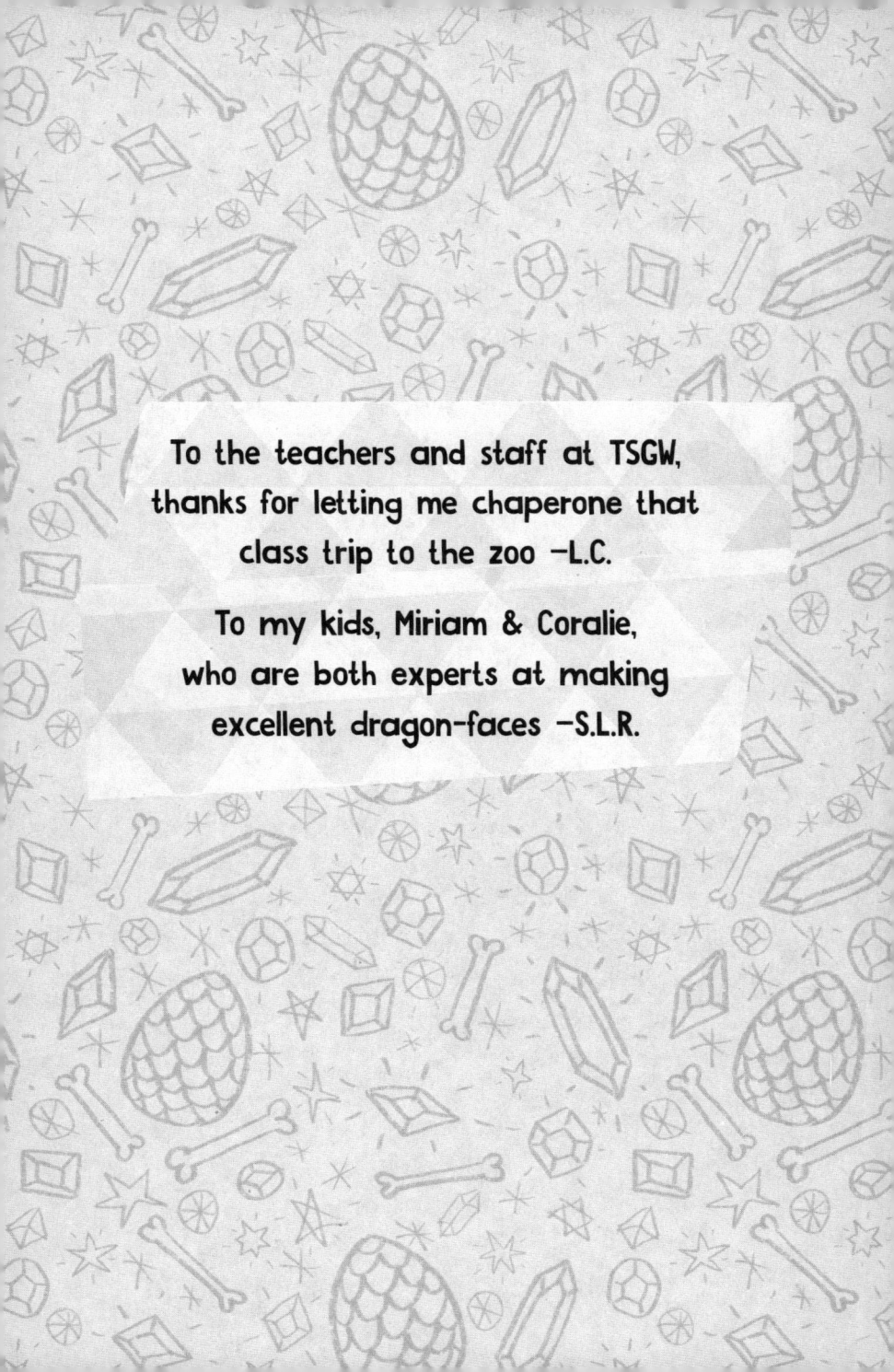

To the teachers and staff at TSGW, thanks for letting me chaperone that class trip to the zoo —L.C.

To my kids, Miriam & Coralie, who are both experts at making excellent dragon-faces —S.L.R.

The SECRET PLAN

1

have been waiting since the first day of school for our class trip to the zoo.

Finally, the day had arrived!

As soon as my alarm went off, I jumped out of bed.

I raced downstairs to the kitchen.

In order to save time on this very important morning, I had gone to sleep the night before wearing my school clothes.

But since my sister, Ariella, says it's gross to sleep in your clothes, I had put my favorite ladybug nightgown on over my school clothes.

I took off the nightgown on my way downstairs and threw it into the laundry bin.

There was no time to waste!

Because I had a *secret plan* for today's trip.

When Ariella was my age, she went on a class trip to the zoo, and she told me that there is a REAL, LIVE DRAGON at the zoo.

At the time, I believed her.

That's because I was young, and I believed everything my family told me.

Now I am older, and I am too smart for them. They're having a hard time dealing with that.

THINGS MY FAMILY TOLD ME THAT I USED TO BELIEVE	HOW I FOUND OUT THE TRUTH
"A tablet is too expensive for a birthday present."	My best friend, Naomi, got a tablet for her birthday.
"If you don't go to bed at eight o'clock, you'll be tired in the morning."	During the Pesach seder, I stayed up until midnight, and I was not tired until the afternoon.

← not even tired!

THINGS MY FAMILY TOLD ME THAT I USED TO BELIEVE	HOW I FOUND OUT THE TRUTH
"We can't get a puppy because your mother is allergic to dogs."	We visited a neighbor who has a dog, and my mother forgot to have allergies.

Now, I investigate things on my own. I am very good at it.

Today, I was going to investigate dragons. Are they real or not?

This time, I would not make up my mind until I had *all the facts.*

I couldn't wait to get started.

Luckily for me, I could get started at breakfast.

My older siblings, Ilan and Ariella, were already sitting at the kitchen table.

Ilan was eating a bowl of bran flakes while reading a book called *The Inter-Diapery Study of Snoringological Boringness.* (Or something like that.)

Ariella was eating a yogurt while looking at her phone.

During breakfast, I tried to interview Ariella about the time she'd seen a dragon at the zoo.

This was a difficult task. First, I had to get her off her phone.

So actually, it was an impossible task.

But I was determined. And if you're determined enough, you can do anything.

That's what my mother always says.

Usually, my mother is talking about homework. She always ruins inspirational sayings by applying them to things like homework.

"Ariella!" I said. "ARIELLA!"

Ariella spoke into her phone. "OMG, that's so cute!"

I leaned over and yelled into her phone: "ARIELLA!"

"Hey!" Ariella said. "I was recording a voice note."

"I have an important question," I said.

"Can it wait a minute?"

"No," I said. "It's really important."

"That's what you said yesterday," Ariella pointed out. "And your question was *Can you buy me a floating bed?*"

"And it's what you said on Shabbat,"

Ilan added. "And your question was *Why aren't there tongue covers so you can eat gross food without tasting it?*"

"But this is crucial for my investigation," I said. "Can you tell me where in the zoo you saw the dragon?"

"It was a long time ago," Ariella said. "I don't remember."

"Do you at least remember what the dragon looked like?"

"Of course," she said. "It was black and green, and it had a red stripe going down its tail."

"Okay," I said. "So now try to remember what everything *around* the dragon looked like."

"Sorry, Miriam. That part didn't stick in my mind."

"Ariella just doesn't want to think about the zoo," Ilan said, "because it will remind her of the *zoo incident!*"

Ariella glared at him. "It doesn't matter where I saw the dragon, because it had *wings*. It could be anywhere by now."

"But I have to start somewhere," I said. "Just try to remember. I know! I could hypnotize you."

"No," Ariella said.

"We could watch videos about how to hypnotize people!"

Ariella looked tempted. Then her phone buzzed, and she said, "Don't be ridiculous, Miriam. And stop bothering me."

Fine. I would investigate *without* her help.

That way she couldn't claim any of the credit when I became world-famous for my discovery about dragons.

In fact, when I got an award for my investigation, I wouldn't let her come to the award ceremony. Not even if she begged me.

"Who is that?" all the news reporters would ask.

"No one," I would say. "No one at all. Try not to step on her while you give me flowers."

When my father came downstairs, I told him that Ariella was refusing to talk to me about the dragon.

"When I'm older," I said, "I'm not going to invite her to my award ceremony, and you had better not make me!"

"What are you going to get an award for?" Ariella asked. "Being annoying?"

"Dad! Ariella called me annoying!"

"I need coffee," my father said.

He always says that.

"Just get coffee at work," Ilan suggested. "It will be quieter there."

My father grinned. "I'm not going to work today!"

Could it be true? I had been hoping and begging, but I hadn't really thought it would happen.

I was almost afraid to ask.

"Are you . . ." I said. "Are you *chaperoning my class trip*?"

"Yes," my father said. "I am!"

"*Thank you!*" This was an *amazing* start to the day. "Thank you, thank you, thank you!"

He grinned even more.

"But just so you know," I added, "I'm going to sit with Naomi on the bus."

2

A SECRET REVEALED

Since my father was chaperoning my class trip, he drove me to school.

That gave me a chance to explain to him how to behave while he was being class chaperone.

RULES FOR CHAPERONES

DO: Bring extra snacks that are just for me.

DO: Pick me up if I'm too short to see something.

DO: Take me secretly away from the group if I need to follow a clue.

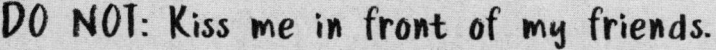

DO NOT: Kiss me in front of my friends.
DO NOT: Hug me in front of my friends.
DO NOT: Call me nicknames. (Ever. But especially in front of my friends.)

And most importantly:
DO NOT: TALK ABOUT DRAGONS.

"I'm going to figure out if there's a real dragon in the zoo," I said. "But I don't want anyone to know about my investigation. They might laugh at me."

"I'm sure no one will laugh at you," he said. "And even if they do, I know you're strong and confident enough to ignore them."

DO NOT: Give me inspirational advice.

eye roll

At school, everyone was jealous because my father was chaperoning the class trip.

"Did he bring extra snacks?" asked my best friend, Naomi.

"Probably," I said.

"Does he have cute nicknames for you?" asked my best enemy, Shimon.

"Definitely not," I said.

"All right, everyone!" called our teacher, Ms. Halpert. "Are you excited for our trip to the zoo?"

"YES!" we said.

"Remember," Ms. Halpert said, "this trip will be a great opportunity to choose an animal for your animal report."

Ugh.

Why do teachers have to make everything so *educational*?

It's like they think that's the whole point of school.

"I already know my animal," Naomi said. "I'm going to choose an elephant!"

"I'm going to choose a penguin," said Shimon.

I felt like everyone was looking at me, waiting to hear what animal I was going to choose.

I didn't want to say it. My plan was *secret*. I had just warned my father not to talk about it!

But the pressure was too intense.

"I'm going to choose a dragon!" I blurted.

Everyone turned to stare at me.

That's when I realized that before, no one had been looking at me at all.

So I could have said nothing.

Oops.

"A dragon?" Shimon laughed. "There's no such thing as dragons."

Now I had no choice but to say things.

"There might be dragons," I said. "My sister saw one."

Shimon crossed his arms. "Where?"

"At the zoo," I said. "The same zoo that we are going to."

A hush fell over the class.

"Is that what the zoo incident was about?" Naomi asked.

"No," I said. "That was something different."

"I'll bet you a million dollars there's no dragon in the zoo," Shimon said.

"Do you have a million dollars?" my father asked.

DO NOT: Ask questions that have nothing to do with anything.

Just then Ms. Halpert told us that we had to get on the bus. It was time to start our trip!

And it was time for *me* to start my investigation.

The NEVER-ENDING BUS RIDE

On the bus, I sat next to Naomi. My father sat across the aisle from me.

"Can I play on your phone?" I asked him.

"No," he said. "I have to answer emails."

He always says that.

Eventually, I started to wonder why we weren't at the zoo yet.

Ms. Halpert had told us the zoo was less than an hour away. And we had definitely been on the bus for eight hours already. Or at least seven.

What if the bus driver was lost?

"Ms. Halpert?" I said.

"Sit down!" the bus driver said.

He always says that.

I thought he should probably concentrate on *where he was going* and not on whether I was standing up for half a second.

I sat down.

"Ms. Halpert?" I said. "How much longer until we get there?"

Ms. Halpert sighed. "Please stop asking that."

She always says that. (Also, Shimon, Naomi, Meira, Eli, and Tzvi had all just asked that, and she didn't sigh at them!)

"Dad?" I said. "How much longer until we get there?"

"My GPS says it's ten more minutes," Dad said.

I love having my father chaperone my class trip.

I waited until ten minutes had passed. But we *still* weren't at the zoo.

"Dad, how much longer?"

"Six minutes and fourteen seconds. Oh wait, now it's six minutes and twelve seconds. Oh wait, now it's six minutes and eleven seconds!"

I stared out the window for as long as I could.

"Dad? How much longer?"

"Four days and sixteen hours. Oh no! We must have taken a wrong turn!"

"*Dad!*"

The bus drove into a parking lot full of other buses.

"Actually," Dad said, "we're here!"

We all thanked the bus driver as we got off the bus.

"We need to stay together and make sure no one gets lost," Ms. Halpert said. "We're going to use the buddy system."

I grabbed Naomi's hand. "We'll be buddies!"

"Can I be your buddy?" Tzvi asked Eli.

"I don't have a buddy!" Becky wailed.

Ms. Halpert held up her hand. "*I'm going to pair you up.*"

She always says that.

And she never pairs me up with Naomi.

Naomi and I looked at each other. We knew what was coming.

But we refused to give up hope.

We held each other's hands. I tried to mentally put a command into Ms. Halpert's mind: *Put me with Naomi. Put me with Naomi. Put me with Naomi.*

"Miriam," Ms. Halpert said, "you go with—"

She paused. Only for a second, but it gave me enough time to think about who I wanted to be put with, in order:

1) Naomi. Obviously.

2) Dassa, because she's quiet and does whatever I want. (So she would probably help me look for dragons.)

3) Not Tzvi, because he thinks I should do whatever _he_ wants. (Which is probably not looking for dragons.)

4) Not Shimon. Obviously.

"—Batsheva," Ms. Halpert finished.

5) Not Batsheva, because she copies everything I do, and it's very annoying.

"All right!" Ms. Halpert said after she was done pairing everyone up. "Remember, it's an important mitzvah to be kind to animals and not cause them pain."

MITZVAH
A good deed that we're commanded to do.

"The zoo has rules to keep the animals safe and happy. Don't try to scare them or feed them, don't get too close to them, and don't tap on any display cases."

"Okay," we all said.

"And remember that this is a public place with a lot of people. I know I can count on you to make a kiddush Hashem."

KIDDUSH HASHEM: If we behave nicely, people will think all religious Jews are nice, and if we behave horribly, people will think all religious Jews behave horribly.

(At least, that's what it means when teachers say it on school trips.)

"And last but not least," she finished, "we're here to have fun!"

Well. That was why everyone else was here.

I had something more important to do.

The INVESTIGATION BEGINS

"Follow me!" Ms. Halpert said. "And while you're looking around, keep your animal report in mind."

"I wish we didn't have to do a report," I said. "I feel like seeing animals is educational enough."

"Yeah!" Batsheva said. "Me too."

"And I don't have time to think about a report," I said. "I have to focus on looking for dragons."

"Me too!" Batsheva said. "I'll help you look!"

Hmm.

Lots of investigators have assistants.

"Okay," I said.

"What should I look for?" Batsheva asked.

Luckily, I had prepared a list of clues. I shared it with her.

FACTS ABOUT DRAGONS	CLUES TO LOOK FOR
Dragons breathe fire.	Try to smell smoke. 
Dragons have claws. 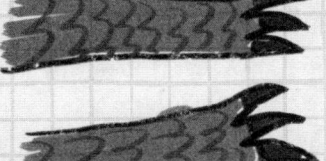	Look for claw marks on trees.
Dragons are the scariest animals in the world. 	Look for terrified people. (I saw some, but it turned out they were terrified of bees.)

FACTS ABOUT DRAGONS	CLUES TO LOOK FOR
Dragons lay eggs that are probably colorful and glittery and maybe have magical powers.	Look for colorful glittery eggs. Or magic.
Dragons live in caves surrounded by treasure and human bones.	The zoo probably doesn't have that much treasure or human bones. But it could definitely have a cave.

As we walked through the zoo, Batsheva and I looked for clues.

I kept getting distracted by the animals.

The zoo had a *lot* of them.

I had expected that.

They mostly smelled bad.

I had not expected that.

I guess animal parents aren't obsessed with showers the way human parents are.

I held my nose as we passed the lemur enclosure.

Batsheva held her nose, too.

I sighed.

Batsheva sighed.

"Miriam!" my father kept saying. "Stand there, I'll take a picture of you!"

Normally I like having my picture taken.

But I was busy looking for a dragon!

"Take selfies of yourself," I suggested.

"I'd rather have a picture of you with the animals."

"Can you just take pictures of the animals without me?"

"No."

"Can you try to get a picture of Shimon picking his nose?"

"No."

Suddenly, Batsheva gasped and grabbed my arm. "Miriam! A clue!"

"Really?" I said. "Where?"

"We just passed a sign that said DRAGON!"

I turned back to look.

"Miriam," Ms. Halpert said. "Stay with the group, please. We're going to see the lions!"

"I have to follow a lead," I explained.

"Miriam," my father said. "Listen to your teacher, and don't argue."

I hate having my father chaperone my class trip.

We had to walk about a million miles to get to the lion enclosure.

My feet hurt and I was hot and my backpack dug into my shoulders.

"Can you carry my backpack?" I asked my father.

"Sure," he said, and took it from me.

"Can you carry my backpack, too?" Batsheva asked. (Of course.)

"Um," he said. "I guess—"

"And mine?" asked Naomi.

"And mine?" asked Shimon.

"Can you carry mine, too?" asked Dassa.

"I'm sorry," my father said. "I can only carry Miriam's backpack."

I love having my father chaperone my class trip.

We spent a lot of time watching the lions.

The lionesses paced back and forth, just like my cat, Pickles, does whenever he's impatient for us to give him dinner.

The male lion looked as grumpy as Pickles does whenever we remind him that he just *had* dinner.

Suddenly, the lion got up and walked toward us!

Everyone shrieked.

The lion came right up to the glass.

He was much bigger than Pickles.

And he looked at me the same way Pickles looks at birds.

I did not like that.

"Let's go," I said.

"You're afraid of the lion!" Shimon said.

"There's nothing wrong with being afraid of lions," my father said. "It's smart of Miriam to be afraid."

I hate having my father chaperone my class trip.

"I am *not* afraid," I said. "But I need to look for clues. And there obviously won't be any dragons near the lion enclosure. Because if there were, there would be no *lions*."

Nobody could argue with that.

We kept walking until we reached the tiger enclosure.

"Look!" Naomi shouted. "That tiger isn't moving. I think it's dead."

"It's not dead," Shimon retorted. "The people who run the zoo don't let dead animals lie around."

I bet it *was* dead.

I bet it was killed by a dragon.

But the dragon had clearly moved on.

"I want to see the rest of the zoo," I said.

"That's a good idea," my father agreed. "Come along, everyone!"

I love having my father chaperone my class trip.

After a bunch more hours, I had seen:

Porcupines sleeping

Koalas sleeping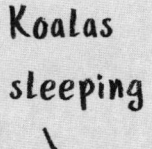

Hippos sleeping

An elephant that was (finally!) not sleeping and was twirling a stick in its trunk. (Naomi was very excited.)

A lot of animals that looked kind of like horses but weren't actually horses and were all eating grass.

okapi

mule zebra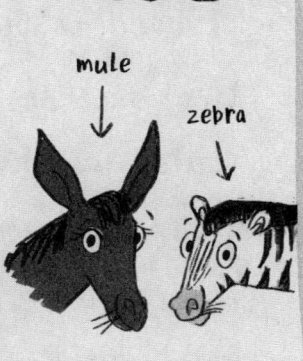

A lot of signs that said STAFF ONLY. (Rude.)

A lot of animals that were hiding from us. (Unless they were hiding from the dragon.)

A cool carousel that we were not allowed to ride on.

(And, apparently, also not allowed to keep asking if we could ride on.)

A lot of gift shops that we were not allowed to buy things at.

(And also not allowed to keep asking if we could buy things at.) (Sheesh.)

Three of the zoo bathrooms because 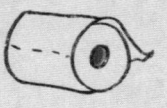   kids kept having to go to the bathroom.

We were watching a bunch of flamingos with very bendy necks when Batsheva suddenly said, "I found another clue!"

She held up something blue and shiny. "Look! A piece of dragon egg!"

I took a closer look.

The shard in her hand glittered slightly.

"That looks like a piece of plastic," Shimon said.

"It's definitely not plastic," Batsheva said. "Touch it!"

I did.

"It feels like a shell from a dragon egg," I said.

"It does to me, too!" Batsheva agreed.

"How do you know what a dragon egg feels like?" Shimon demanded.

"Sometimes," I said, "an investigator has to trust her instincts."

5

The PROBLEM with DEMOCRACY

"When are we going back to school?" Shimon asked. "I'm so hot!"

"I'm hot, too!" said Batsheva.

And I thought it was bad when she was only copying *me*!

"I'm hot, too!" said Avi.

"Me too!" said Naomi.

This was a disaster.

We couldn't go back to school!

I hadn't found the dragon yet. I had barely even found any clues!

♡ CLUES FOUND SO FAR

* Sign that says DRAGON (possibly)
* Tiger that was possibly killed by a dragon
* Animals that were possibly hiding from a dragon
* Pieces of (possible) dragon eggshells

"Shouldn't we eat first?" I asked. "Watching the zebras eat grass made me hungry."

"Yeah," Batsheva said. "It made me hungry, too."

"Passing all the food stands made *me* hungry!" Shimon said.

"They're not kosher," Naomi told him.

"Some of the ice cream is kosher," he said.

"Really?" we all said.

"We're not eating ice cream," Ms. Halpert said. "We'll have lunch soon. In the meantime, let's sit down and have some of the snacks from your backpacks."

My parents had packed me cut-up melon for a snack.

But Batsheva had a bag of barbecue potato chips.

"I love barbecue potato chips," I said.

"Me too," Batsheva said.

"But aren't you afraid you'll get a stomachache if you eat the whole bag by yourself?"

"Miriam," my father said. "Eat your own snack."

I hate having my father chaperone my class trip.

"We have time for one more activity before lunch," Ms. Halpert said. "Then we'll get back on the bus."

Oh no!

My time was running out!

"We can go see the swans at the pond," Ms. Halpert said, "or we can go to the monkey house, or we can go to the Reptile Discovery Center."

The *Reptile Discovery Center*!

Of course!

That's where the dragon would be.

FACTS ABOUT DRAGONS	CLUES TO LOOK FOR
Dragons are cold-blooded reptiles.	Check out the Reptile Discovery Center!

"Let's go see the reptiles!" I said. "They're so cool! Literally!" I cracked up.

No one else did.

"Because reptiles are cold-blooded," I explained.

Still no one laughed.

"I think that's a funny joke," I said.

I waited for Batsheva to say *Me too*.

She did not.

"Snakes are gross," Shimon said. "Let's go to the monkey house."

"Yeah!" a bunch of kids shouted.

"Let's see the swans!" Batsheva said.

"We only have time for one activity," Ms. Halpert told us.

"Great!" I said. "So we'll go to the Reptile Discovery Center."

"We'll vote on it," Ms. Halpert said.

WHAT?

I *hate* voting.

Other people *never* want to do what I want to do.

"Let's go to the reptiles!" I shouted, and held up my hand.

Batsheva did not hold up hers.

"Sorry," she whispered. "I really want to see the swans."

Some assistant.

But Naomi, who is a good and loyal friend, held up her hand.

So did Eli, Dassa, and Shlomo.

I started to have hope.

"Dad!" I hissed.

"I'm a chaperone," he said. "I can't vote."

"Of course you can!" I said. "Chaperones have rights, too."

"Really?" he said. "I hadn't noticed."

I had no idea what he was talking about.

"Of course you have rights!" I said. "Use your rights to vote for what *I* want!"

"All right," he said. "I vote for the Reptile Discovery Center, too."

I love having my father chaperone my class trip.

I turned to the rest of my class.

There were eighteen of us, and five kids raising their hands, so in order to get us to the Reptile Discovery Center, I needed, um . . . a lot more.

(This wasn't *math* class, okay?)

"Who wants to see the swans?" Ms. Halpert asked.

Six kids raised their hands.

I started to panic.

How could I change their minds?

What if . . . What if I told them about the *zoo incident*?

Ariella would be really mad at me.

But it was Ariella's fault I had barely any clues! If she'd told me that the dragon was in the Reptile Discovery Center, I might have solved the case already.

Then again . . . Ariella had promised me she would never tell anyone about the *waterslide incident*. And she never had.

I opened my mouth. I closed it.

I couldn't do it. I couldn't betray my sister.

Even though she totally deserved it.

I was just too noble.

I would not tell my class about the zoo incident.

I would keep my silence forever.

The ZOO INCIDENT

I can tell *you*, though.

That's different.

Ariella once watched a video about "the language of swans." The video was all about how you could use swan body language to say hello to swans and make them like you.

I don't think that sort of thing even works with people, so I don't know why it would work with swans, but Ariella would not listen to my advice.

The next time we went to the zoo, Ariella immediately insisted that we go to the pond where the swans were.

The swans looked beautiful and peaceful.

Ariella started doing the swan language she'd learned about in the video.

She made eye contact with a swan. She moved her head up and down.

Everyone stared at her.

I tried to pretend I didn't know her.

The swan swam closer.

Ariella held out her hand.

The swan suddenly rose out of the water, wings flapping, and jabbed at her with its beak!

Ariella screamed and stepped back. The swan got out of the water and went after her!

I guess whatever she said in swan language made it *really* mad.

Ariella turned and ran.

WHAT ARIELLA PROBABLY SAID TO THE SWAN

Your feathers are dirty.

Your neck is not long enough.

I thought you were a duck.

The swan ran after her. It chased her all along the pond, hissing and flapping its wings and jabbing at her with its beak.

"Help! *Help!*" Ariella screamed.

THINGS I NOW KNOW ABOUT SWANS

Swans look <u>really</u> big when they open their wings wide.

Swans have long, graceful necks that are also really long (but not as graceful) when they use them as weapons.

My parents went running after Ariella.

Everyone was screaming.

Ariella ran as fast as she could.

ANOTHER THING I NOW KNOW ABOUT SWANS

They run fast.

The swan jabbed the back of Ariella's legs.

Ariella fell face-first into the pond.

The swan floated away, looking beautiful and peaceful.

Ariella, dripping wet, walked over to my parents.

Then we had to go home and I never got to see the rest of the zoo. But no one had any sympathy for me. All they cared about was Ariella.

As usual.

"All right!" Ms. Halpert said, when the voting was over. "Looks like the monkey house got the most votes."

I *hate* democracy.

In the monkey house, a gorilla was taking a nap on a branch.

"That gorilla looks like a big stuffed animal," Shimon said. "I bet it's fake."

"I bet a bunch of the animals in the zoo are fake," Eli said.

The gorilla got up and swung itself onto a different branch.

"See?" I told Shimon. "That's what's called *evidence*. The gorilla is real!"

"You still don't have evidence that *dragons* are real," Shimon said.

"That's your fault," I said. "*You* voted against the Reptile Discovery Center."

I was talking to Shimon, but I was also secretly talking to Batsheva. I was still mad at her for not voting with me.

She didn't seem to notice, though. She had gone to look at the chimpanzees.

The chimpanzees were not napping. They were jumping and swinging and having a ton of fun.

One of them peeled a banana!

Chimpanzees are smart.

Then it ate the banana peel.

So maybe they aren't that smart.

One chimpanzee swung along the ceiling and slid down a pole.

"That looks like fun," I said. "If I was a chimpanzee, I would do that all the time."

"Yeah," Batsheva said. "I would, too."

I ignored her.

One of the chimpanzees started playing with a ball.

Suddenly, another chimpanzee jumped on the first chimpanzee and tried to pull the ball away!

The first chimpanzee ran across the floor, holding the ball under one arm.

The other chimpanzee chased it.

The two chimpanzees climbed straight up the walls and started swinging across the ceiling.

All the kids in my class started cheering and taking sides.

"I want the first chimpanzee to win!" I said. "I like that one better!"

Batsheva opened her mouth.

"You'd better not say you like that one better, too!" I said.

"Miriam!" my father exclaimed. "Why would you say something like that?"

"Sorry," I muttered to Batsheva.

I hate having my father chaperone my class trip.

"LOOK!" Shimon shouted. "THAT GORILLA IS POOPING!"

Most of my class wanted to spend more time watching the gorilla poop. But Ms. Halpert insisted that it was time to leave.

So much for all that talk about enjoying the zoo.

I was okay with leaving, though. There were obviously no dragons in the monkey house.

Also, gorilla poop smells *really* terrible.

Outside the monkey house, I tried to think of a way to continue my investigation.

"Can some of us go to the Reptile Discovery Center instead of eating lunch?" I asked. "I'm not hungry."

As I said it, my stomach grumbled.

"Oh!" I said, looking around. "Was that a lion?"

"I think you need food," my father said.

He always says that.

"I really, really want to go see the reptiles," I said. "If I don't go to the Reptile Discovery Center, this whole trip was for nothing!"

"Come on, Miriam. That's not true," my father said.

"It *is* true!" I said. "Let's go for just a minute. Please?"

"I'm chaperoning the whole class. I can't leave to take one kid somewhere. It wouldn't be fair to everyone else."

"I want to go to the Reptile Discovery Center, too!" Batsheva said.

Hmm. Maybe she was a good assistant after all.

I smiled at her.

She smiled back.

My father went to talk to Ms. Halpert.

I watched them anxiously.

"What do you think they're talking about?" I asked Batsheva.

"I think he's asking her if he can take us to see the reptiles," Batsheva said.

"I hope you're right," I said.

"What else could they be talking about?" Batsheva asked.

I could think of a million things.

THINGS ADULTS LIKE TO TALK ABOUT

* Stuff people said in the news
* Their work
* "Funny" things that happened a gazillion years ago (that weren't funny then either)
* How kids should spend less time on screens

Finally, my father came back.

"All right," he said. "We can go to the Reptile Discovery Center for a few—"

"YAY!" I said. "Thank you! A few hours?"

"A few minutes," my father said. "And while I'm in charge, you have to do exactly as I say."

"Really?" I said. "What if you say I have to jump into the crocodile cage?"

My father sighed.

"What if you say I have to let all the snakes out?"

"Let's just go to the Reptile Discovery Center," my father said.

I love having my father chaperone my class trip.

The REPTILE DISCOVERY CENTER (YAY!)

There were clues EVERYWHERE in the Reptile Discovery Center.

CLUES

The doorway of the Reptile Discovery Center has fancy designs that look exactly like dragon scales.

The small lizards all look mad, probably because they don't like being kept near a dragon.

"I think lizards always look mad," my father said. "That's just how their mouths are."

A lot of the snakes are hiding under rocks, probably because they're hiding from the dragon.

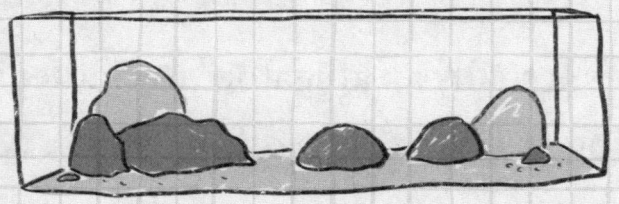

"It says here that snakes hibernate underground," my father said.

The crocodile was not moving AT ALL and also did not look real.

It was definitely a statue of a crocodile. That they made after a dragon ate the real crocodile.

"It's actually an alligator," my father said, reading the sign. "The difference is . . ."

I did not listen as he explained the difference. I was not here to investigate crocodiles or alligators.

We kept walking. We saw an iguana that also looked fake, but like it was made by someone who wasn't very good at making fakes. We turned a corner.

And then I saw the BEST CLUE EVER.

It was a sign.

And the sign said:

I was so excited that I started jumping up and down.

"Where's the dragon?!" I yelled.

A man smiled at me. He was wearing a shirt that said ZOO VOLUNTEER.

"You have to go outside to see the dragon," he said.

Outside the Reptile Discovery Center, there was a fence, and behind the fence, there was—

I stopped.

I stared.

The animal behind the fence was huge and lizardy with leathery gray skin.

It had sharp claws.

Its head was long and pointed.

"The sign lied!" I said. "This is not a dragon!"

"Sure it is!" my father said. "Look at *this* sign!"

I looked at the sign on the fence.

It said KOMODO DRAGON.

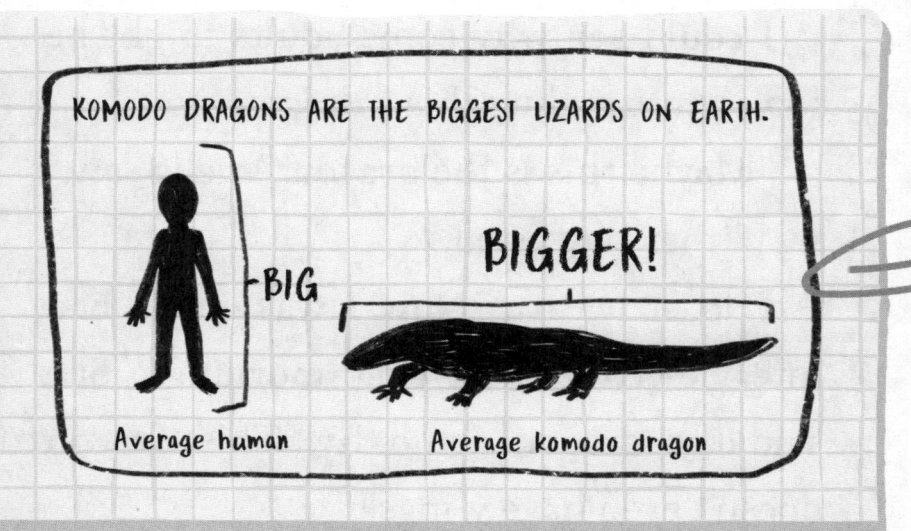

I read the rest of the sign.

That did sound like dragons.

I could see why some adults might be fooled into calling this a dragon.

"Maybe this is the dragon Ariella saw," my father suggested.

"No, it wasn't." Now I was glad I had interviewed Ariella that morning. "She said the dragon could fly! This dragon doesn't even have wings!"

COMPARISON OF REAL DRAGONS AND KOMODO DRAGONS

	Real Dragons	Komodo Dragons
COLD-BLOODED REPTILES	Yes	Yes
BIG AND SCARY	Yes	Yes, according to the sign. (At the zoo, it looked kind of asleep.)
HAVE CLAWS	Yes	Yes
LAY EGGS	Yes	Yes

COMPARISON OF REAL DRAGONS AND KOMODO DRAGONS

	Real Dragons	Komodo Dragons
ACTUALLY MOVE	Yes	Only its eyelids, at least while I was there.
HAVE WINGS	Yes	No
BREATHE FIRE	Yes	Probably not. The fence did not look fireproof.

"I guess we should go back to the lunch area," I said, trying not to cry.

"Wait," Batsheva said. She bent and picked up something from the ground.

It was another piece of dragon egg!

"Look there," my father said, pointing at a small pond.

A bit of blue was floating on the water.

"What do you think those are?" my father asked.

"It's a trail of broken dragon shells!" I exclaimed. "I think we should follow it."

"Me too!" Batsheva said.

"Miriam!" my father shouted. "Wait!"

But I could not wait.

THE TRUTH was right there. And I was about to discover it!

DRAGON!

We raced around the pond.

A few turtles poked their heads above the surface, then saw the dragon eggshells in our hands and immediately went back underwater.

I almost bumped into a woman who was walking toward us.

She was also wearing a ZOO VOLUNTEER shirt.

"Hello!" she said. "Can I help you find something?"

"We're looking for a dragon," I explained.

"Right back there!" She pointed the way we had come.

"Not a Komodo dragon," I said. "A real dragon."

"Oh, you're so cute!" she said.

WHAT ADULTS USUALLY MEAN WHEN THEY SAY "YOU'RE CUTE"*

You're saying something silly.

I'm going to pretend I like your costume even though I don't.

You just used a big word, and you pronounced it wrong.

*Except for my grandmother—when she says I'm cute, she actually means "You're cute."

"A Komodo dragon *is* a real dragon," the zoo volunteer told us.

"We're looking for a dragon that breathes fire and flies," Batsheva explained.

"Ooh. Well, that would be a fire hazard. We can't have one of those at the zoo . . ." Then she leaned down and whispered, ". . . *officially.*"

I stared at her.

"Keep going the way you're going."

She winked and walked away.

"Girls?" my father said. "We really should go back."

"I just need one more minute," Batsheva said.

"Me too!" I said.

We followed the eggshells along the pond.

We passed a bunch of tiny swimming turtles.

We passed a giant turtle that was bigger than me.

We passed a crocodile or alligator.

(I was much too focused on dragons to care which.)

Just as we reached the end of the pond, I felt a blast of heat.

Batsheva gasped. "Look up!"

I heard a *whoosh*ing sound from above.

I looked up.

AND I SAW IT.

It was huge, with two widespread wings. After a split second, it vanished behind a cloud.

Batsheva and I were still staring at the sky when my father caught up to us.

"Hey," he said, sniffing the air. "Where is that smell of smoke coming from?"

"From the dragon!" I said.

"It was gigantic!" Batsheva added. "It had two scaly wings. It was black and green."

"Black and green?" I repeated. Ariella had also said the dragon was black and green! But I had never told Batsheva that!

This was proof.

My father laughed. "Black and green, like the dragon in that fantasy series Ariella is always reading?"

I focused on Batsheva. "You're sure it was black and green?"

"Well..." Batsheva bit her lip.

My heart sank.

"Mostly black and green," Batsheva said. "It also had one red stripe going down its tail."

10

The ANIMAL REPORT

KOMODO DRAGONS
By Miriam and Batsheva

Dragons are real, and we know they are real because we both saw one, and so did Miriam's sister, Ariella, and the dragons we saw looked exactly the same.

But Ariella refused to be interviewed for this report.

And when we called the zoo's information office, they said there are no fire-breathing dragons in the zoo "or anywhere else, as far as we know."

Of course, that's what they <u>have</u> to say.

They also claimed they could not tell us who "the volunteer with the brown hair" is.

Which we find very suspicious.

So we don't have absolute proof.

<u>Yet.</u>

But the report is due tomorrow, so we are doing it on Komodo dragons, which are not really dragons.

We are writing this report under protest.

But please give us a good grade anyhow.

Komodo dragons are only called "dragons" because they are very big lizards and also are dangerous. They do not breathe fire. Or fly. Or have any magical powers.

They are pretty cool, though.

If they were called "Komodo killer lizards," they would be cooler. Because then people would not compare them to dragons and decide they are not as cool as dragons.

They are ~~carinvoris~~ ~~carnivours~~ carnivores, which means they eat meat and hunt other animals.

They will also kill and eat each other. (That part is not so cool, but it is true.)

They have poison in their mouths. (Or maybe it is dangerous bacteria. But poison sounds cooler.)

Komodo dragons are one of the rarest lizards. There are fewer than six thousand Komodo dragons in the whole world.

But they are not as rare as real dragons, because there is only one real dragon that has ever been seen (by us, and by Ariella).

Komodo dragons' stomachs can stretch really really really big.

A Komodo dragon can eat a whole water buffalo! (Apparently those <u>are</u> real—my brother showed me in a book.)

Having a water buffalo in its stomach makes a Komodo dragon super heavy. So if it needs to run, it will throw up everything it ate and then run.

That is probably very gross.

Adult Komodo dragons are ugly. Baby Komodo dragons are cute. But I bet they don't like it when adults call them cute. (Except maybe if the adult is their grandmother.)

An adult Komodo dragon probably making the babies clean up the eggshells even though they were just born.

Komodo dragons live about thirty years, and the females can have babies all by themselves even after being alone in a zoo for years, which is called ~~parthen pathre~~ parthenogenesis. We don't know enough science to explain that yet. But we think even a real dragon can't do that, so that is cool.

But not as cool as breathing fire.

Komodo dragons live only on a few islands in Indonesia. One of these islands is called Komodo Island.

Komodo dragons weren't formally discovered by the rest of the world until 1912! Until then, most people had only heard rumors about them.

So it's <u>very possible</u> that another kind of dragon will be discovered next.

Probably by <u>US</u>.

Where Do Stories About Dragons COME FROM?

Dragons show up in the legends of almost every culture in the world.

In the Western world, dragons are usually depicted as scary creatures that fly and breathe fire.

But dragons come in many forms!

A FEW TYPES OF DRAGONS

Western Europe

Scary, dangerous, and greedy.

In the oldest known English-language poem, <u>Beowulf</u>, the hero fights a dragon who is burning down everything in sight because someone stole one of its treasures.

A FEW TYPES OF DRAGONS

China

Good, beautiful, and helpful.

Chinese emperors wore robes with dragon patterns sewn on them. No one except the emperor was allowed to have dragons on their clothes!

A FEW TYPES OF DRAGONS

Aboriginal tribes of Australia

Associated with water—not fire!

Some of these dragons have been called <u>rainbow serpents</u> in English because of the belief that they create rainbows as they move.

Ancient Aztecs

Worshipped a god named Quetzalcoatl, a huge feathered serpent that looks a lot like a dragon.

You probably can't guess how to pronounce that! It's KWET-SUHL-KUH-WAHT-UHL.

And there are many, many other types of dragons!

The strangest thing about these dragon stories is that they appear even in cultures that had no contact with one another. How did all these people separately come up with the idea of dragons?

That is another case that is still open!

Here are a few theories:

People found dinosaur bones and thought they must be dragon bones. (But there are dragon stories even in places that have no dinosaur bones.)

Early humans lived in constant fear of predators—many of which were either very large, attacked from the air, or had scales. Dragon stories came out of that fear.

Dragon stories grew out of stories about <u>real</u> animals like iguanas, alligators, and...

Komodo dragons!

(Which are all pretty scary if you see them outside a zoo.)

OR All these people knew about dragons, because

DRAGONS ARE REAL!